Other stories by Marjorie Weinman Sharmat:

From the *Nate the Great* series

Nate the Great
Nate the Great Goes Undercover
Nate the Great and the Lost List
Nate the Great and the Phony Clue
Nate the Great and the Sticky Case
Nate the Great and the Missing Key
Nate the Great and the Snowy Trail
Nate the Great and the Fishy Prize
Nate the Great Stalks Stupidweed
Nate the Great and the Boring Beach Bag
Nate the Great Goes Down in the Dumps
Nate the Great and the Halloween Hunt
Nate the Great and the Musical Note
      (by Marjorie Weinman Sharmat and Craig Sharmat)
Nate the Great and the Stolen Base
Nate the Great and the Pillowcase
      (by Marjorie Weinman Sharmat and Rosalind Weinman)
Nate the Great and the Mushy Valentine
Nate the Great and the Tardy Tortoise
      (by Marjorie Weinman Sharmat and Craig Sharmat)
Nate the Great and the Crunchy Christmas
      (by Marjorie Weinman Sharmat and Craig Sharmat)
Nate the Great Saves the King of Sweden
Nate the Great and Me: The Case of the Fleeing Fang
Nate the Great and the Monster Mess
      (illustrated by Martha Weston)

From the *Olivia Sharp* series
      (by Marjorie Weinman Sharmat and Mitchell Sharmat)

The Pizza Monster
The Princess of the Fillmore Street School
The Sly Spy
The Green Toenails Gang

DIRTY TRICKS

Marjorie Weinman Sharmat
author of *Nate the Great*

illustrated by Veronica Jones

Random House New York

For all of Dudley Sharmat's loyal fans
who saw the dedications of books #2 and #3
and are now eagerly awaiting his movie:
Unfortunately, Dudley's producers gave him
a simply terrible dressing room,
so he went on strike and the movie is delayed.
Dudley regrets any inconveniences
this may have caused.
—M.W.S.

Text copyright © 2000 by Marjorie Weinman Sharmat
Illustrations copyright © 2000 by Veronica Jones
Cover art copyright © 2000 by Paul Blumstein
All rights reserved under International and Pan-American Copyright Conventions.
Published in the United States by Random House, Inc., New York, and
simultaneously in Canada by Random House of Canada Limited, Toronto.

www.randomhouse.com/kids

Library of Congress Cataloging-in-Publication Data
Sharmat, Marjorie Weinman.
Dirty tricks / by Marjorie Weinman Sharmat ; illustrated by Veronica Jones.
p.   cm. — (Duz Shedd ; 4)
Sequel to: Genghis Khan: dog-gone Hollywood.
SUMMARY: Fred is excited that his movie star dog Duz, also known as Genghis Khan,
is about to release an exercise video for other dogs, but then the heinous Veronica Slye
comes out with an imitation video of her monster cat.
ISBN 0-679-86954-9 (trade) — ISBN 0-679-96954-3 (lib. bdg.)
[1. Dogs—Fiction. 2. Motion pictures—Production and direction—Fiction.] I. Jones,
Veronica, ill. II. Title. III. Series: Sharmat, Marjorie Weinman. Duz Shedd ; 4.
PZ7.S5299De 2000
[Fic]—dc21   99-34762

Printed in the United States of America November 2000
10 9 8 7 6 5 4 3 2 1

A Duz Shedd Story

My dog won an Oscar for Best Actor in a movie.

That's right. My *dog*.

He won over four other actors. None of them have tails or paws. Or fleas.

My dog's movie-star name is Genghis Khan.

His real name is Duz.

That, of course, is short for "Does he bite?"

He doesn't.

In fact, Duz has become a role model for dogs everywhere.

People want their dogs to be just like Duz.

They want to know how Duz does what he does.

They wanted to know even before Duz won his Oscar.

But now they *really* want to know.

One day a few months ago, Duz's agent, Zero Fogg, said, "Duz should make a video."

"A video?" I asked.

"Yes. A video for dogs. I've had offers. But now's the time to do it. Trust me. Fred Shedd, have I ever given you or your folks bad advice?"

My best friend, Pamela Brinkman, was sitting there listening. So were my parents. We were hanging out on the huge patio of our Hollywood home.

Pamela piped up, "This may come as a

shock to you, but dogs don't buy videos. They don't have a whole lot of spending money."

"But their owners do," Zero said.

"What could Duz do on the video?" my father asked.

"Good question," Zero said.

I looked at Duz. He was leaping around the patio. His leap is famous.

"Awesome leap," Zero said.

"Duz sure loves to exercise," I said.

Zero stared into space and licked his lips. Suddenly *he* leaped into the air. "Yes, yes, YES!" he said.

"Yes, yes, yes what?" I asked.

"Duz could do an *exercise* video. He could show dogs his exercises, give them tips, help them stay in shape. We could call it *Shape Up with Duz!*"

"Catchy," Pamela said.

"There you go," Zero said.

"Not so fast," I said. "Can we give most of the money we make to dog shelters? Duz would like that."

Duz raised an ear. He wagged his tail.

Zero patted Duz. "Inspired idea. It'll be great P.R. I'll work out the details."

It took fourteen phone calls and three days for Zero to make the deal.

Duz started to practice for his video. His coach, Ms. Muddlewolf, worked with him. She had plenty of baloney with her. That's what she always used to help train Duz. He loves the stuff!

Then the big day came. It was time to

go to the studio to shoot the video.

The news was all over the radio, newspapers, and TV for days. Everyone wanted to watch Duz make the video. We got phone calls, letters, faxes.

"No, no, no!" Zero said, tossing some of the papers into the air. "We don't want people hanging around. This dog was kidnapped once. From a movie set full of people. This time I've hired guards. Top security. If only I could have gotten the Secret Service."

"They're pretty busy," Pamela said.

My parents, Pamela, Zero, Ms. Muddle-wolf, and I went off to the video shoot. Duz's chauffeur, Fritz, drove us in our limo.

When we arrived, I counted twenty-five security guards.

"Show biz," Pamela said. "I love it, I love it."

Duz sniffed every guard.

2

Inside, lots of people were running around, getting things set up.

The stage was flooded with bright lights. And in the background there were bones and kibbles made of flashing neon lights.

Pamela gasped. "Flashing *kibbles?* Now I know why I moved to Hollywood."

Duz was backstage, getting ready. Combed, brushed, massaged, and polished. He had to look his very best.

Or maybe his very worst.

Duz had become famous because he's so ugly-looking.

Suddenly he appeared on the stage. In gold satin tights.

He looked ready and happy.

The taping started.

"Here comes the music," I whispered to Pamela.

Duz's video theme song began playing. It's called "Do the Duzzy."

"Thump! Bump! Don't be fuzzy, do the Duzzy. Wiggle, jiggle!"

Duz raised an ear. He scrunched his nose.

Then he thumped. He bumped. He wiggled. He jiggled.

The song kept going.

"Wag that tail! Fetch that mail!"

Duz wagged his tail.

Pamela poked me. "Tail-wagging is an *exercise?*"

"Sure," I said. "Do you want the tail to just *hang* there? Doing *nothing?* A tail is meant to swoosh, whoosh, swoosh..."

"I get it," Pamela said.

Zero poked me. "It's time to fetch."

I clenched my teeth.

"What's the matter?" Zero asked.

"See the pile of mail at the corner of the stage? Duz has to go fetch it in his teeth," I said.

Zero snickered. "So? Fred Shedd, my young friend, even I could do that in my teeth."

My father leaned over. "It's not easy for Duz. He only likes to fetch shoes. Before we adopted him, somebody must have trained him to fetch shoes."

"But at least he's particular," my

mother said. "The shoes have to be shiny and smell new and have tassels."

"Why wasn't I told this?" Zero said. "It should have been in my contract with this dog. Does he have any more secrets...a wife, children?"

"There he goes," Pamela said. "He's after the mail."

Duz ran toward the pile of mail. Then he stopped and looked down.

"Uh-oh, one of the cameramen is wearing shiny new shoes," I said. "And Duz sees them."

Zero was in shock. "You mean he goes after shoes *on* feet?"

"I forgot to mention that," I said. "Wait! Now Duz is looking straight ahead."

"No wonder," Pamela said, pointing toward a door. "A delivery guy just came in. With bowls of dog treats. See him? He's wearing a CALL-A-KIBBLE jacket and cap."

Zero yelled, "Who called for dog food? Get it out of here!"

The delivery guy walked away.

"We have to start all over again," Zero said. "And you with the new shoes. Please remove them. Thank you."

Duz started again.

"Stop!" yelled the director. "Duz's tights are wrinkled. That will never do. Costume change."

My mother whispered to me, "Fred, you are going to be a very old man before this is finished."

Duz started again. In a new pair of gold satin tights.

He got to the fetch part.

"Hold your breath," Pamela said. "He's going for the mail!"

Duz fetched the mail in his teeth. I felt like applauding.

The song went on, *"Did you fetch? Now you stretch."*

Duz bent and stretched.

Back and forth. Back and forth.

Then the song was over.

"Now what?" my mother asked.

"Watch!" I said.

Duz looked straight ahead. He opened his mouth. Slowly.

Then "GRRRRRRRRRRRRRRRrrr!!!!!!"

Out came the famous Genghis growl.

"Is that a mouth exercise?" my mother asked.

"No," I said. "It's a message from Duz to dogs everywhere. It will be flashed across the video screen in words for people to read."

"So what does it mean?" Pamela asked.

"It means

BE PROUD YOU CAN GROWL.
BE PROUD YOU CAN GRRRR.
BE PROUD THAT MOST FLEAS
WANT TO LIVE IN YOUR FUR.

BE PROUD YOU'RE A DOG!
EXERCISE. EAT WELL.
AND ABOVE ALL,
DON'T BE A COUCH CANINE."

"He said that in just one growl?" my father asked.

"Duz is a very fast talker," I said.

The taping was over.

Zero clapped his hands. "Your dog, my client, is pure talent," he said. "He was fantastic."

"So now the dog shelters will get a lot of money," I said. "The video will be a giant success, right?"

"Unless something goes wrong," Zero said. "This is Hollywood. You never know who's lurking around the corner, ready to make trouble."

The *Shape Up with Duz* video was sure to be a hit. I just *knew* it.

Here's what we had going for us:

Duz is famous.

Duz is a role model.

Duz is sweet.

Duz is talented.

Duz's video will help other dogs.

Zero popped into my house one day with another reason. "This video has great advance word of mouth," he said. "The public knows it's coming. They can't wait!"

"It's been a long wait," I said. "Isn't it ready yet?"

"Not so fast," Zero said. "There's a tiny glitch. Duz needs to redo a bit of the video. Just a titch."

"A titch of a glitch? What glitch?"

"Duz raised an ear when he wiggled."

"But his fans love it when he raises an ear. He's *known* for raising his ear."

"But not when he *wiggles*," Zero said. "They just don't match up."

Zero groaned.

"This could delay us for weeks," he said. "I hate delays. Timing is everything. The video should come out while Duz is still hot from his Oscar win."

"Still hot? You mean Duz is going to cool off?"

"That's what it's all about in Hollywood," Zero said. "Hot. Cool. Lukewarm.

Stone cold. Hollywood is just one big weather report."

Zero sighed. "Well, at least this gives me extra time to book Duz on some TV shows. We have to launch the video with strong publicity."

"Just a minute," I said. "First there was a movie, then an Oscar race, then the video. When is Duz *ever* going to rest?"

Zero looked at his watch and laughed. "He has at least an hour."

"Very funny," I said.

4

After Zero went home, I said to Duz, "We are now officially going to rest. Do nothing."

Duz wagged his tail.

I got the TV remote and sat down on the couch. "Let's watch a sort of *nothing* TV program. Okay?"

I motioned for Duz to come up on the couch.

He didn't come.

"Oh, I get it," I said. "You don't want to be a couch canine. Well, it's okay for a few minutes."

Duz jumped up and snuggled next to me. It was nice. Just the two of us with nothing to do.

"You're my dog, I'm your boy," I said. "Remember when I found you as a stray? That was my lucky day."

Duz snuggled closer.

I pointed the remote at the TV screen. "Let's go channel-surfing," I said. "I'll press the button. Bark when you see something you want to watch."

Click!

A woman was selling jewelry. "Ladies, this ruby ring..."

Click!

A man was batting a baseball. "Tendilla is up at the plate..."

Click!

The President was sitting in the Oval Office. "My fellow Americans..."

Click! Duz is *very* picky.

A lady was sitting on a chair on a stage. "My cat's video..."

"RUFF! RUFF! RUFF!"

"Duz, you found something you like?"

"GRRRRRRRRRRRRRRRrrr!"

"Something you *don't* like?"

I looked back at the screen. I *knew* that lady. She was still talking.

"I want you to meet the star of the video *Shape Up with Geca.* My cat, the fitness feline herself...Geca!"

"What?" Now I was paying attention to the screen.

A big, ugly cat ran onto the stage and jumped on the lady's shoulder.

Duz looked at me.

"I know," I said. "It's Veronica Slye, the woman who kidnapped you. And her monster cat. She wanted that horrible cat

23

to replace you in your movie."

"GRRRRRRRRRRRRRRRrrr."

"Right. And now she's got a *shape-up* video. First she steals you. Now she's stealing our video idea."

I looked at the screen again. Veronica was on a talk show. And she was doing plenty of talking.

"My cat could have been a movie star," she said. "But now she's something better. A video star. Her video will help cats everywhere to be healthy and fit."

I clicked off the TV.

"What are we going to do, Duz?" I asked.

"GRRRRRRRRRRRRRRRRRrrr."

That sounded good to me.

5

The call came fast. I knew it would.

Zero was on the phone, fuming. "That monster cat. That monster *copy*cat! But *her* video is on the market and ours isn't."

"How did Veronica have a chance to do a video?" I asked. "She was sentenced to work at a dog shelter for kidnapping Duz."

"Yeah, but she doesn't live there twenty-four hours a day," Zero said. "A good thing for the dogs she doesn't."

"This is an awful mess for Duz," I said. "He tried so hard. But now everybody will think his video is just a copy of Geca's. They won't want it."

Zero started to yell. "That crazy cat will capture the animal fitness market! She jumped in ahead of us."

"What can we do?"

"Something big," Zero said. "It has to be something really big. Something that proves that our Duz—the mighty Genghis Khan—is an immortal Hollywood legend. And to own his video is to own a piece of Hollywood history."

"That *does* sound big," I said.

"Yeah, I'm gonna cream that cat!"

Zero hung up.

I hoped he would call back soon.

A week went by. Duz was rushed back to the studio to redo his wiggle. Unfortunately, the director was wearing bright, new tasseled shoes.

Duz decided to fetch.

His video was taking longer to make than a movie! Now they were working day and night to get it ready to sell to the world.

Then—at last—the day came. The video was ready.

But Zero still didn't call.

Pamela did. She kept calling. And one day she came over to my house with a package.

"Guess what I've got," she said. "The cat video."

"I don't want to see it," I said.

"You have to see it," Pamela said. "You have to be strong and look at it."

"Have you seen it?"

"No, I just bought it. I had to stand in line. Idiots. Buying this stupid video."

"In line? A long line?"

"Well, yes. But the people didn't look very smart."

"How can you tell?"

"Their eyes were dull, their bodies drooped, their hair—"

"Forget it. Nice try. They were buying Geca's video. That's what counts."

"Play it," Pamela ordered.

Pamela and I sat down to watch the video I didn't want to see. Duz was in another room. Good for him.

There was Geca in silver satin tights. And in back of her, saucers of milk made of flashing neon lights.

"They copied what we did!" Pamela said. "Except that it's catty."

It got a whole lot worse. There was a song. The music sounded a lot like ours. But the words were different. An awful

rhyme about how it's better to purr than to grrr.

Geca did some leaping exercises. She scratched a scratching post. She did somersaults. Then she stood and gave a loud purr while a message flashed across the screen:

BE PROUD YOU'RE A CAT.
BE PROUD YOU CAN PURR.
BE PROUD YOU'RE TOO CLEAN
TO HAVE FLEAS IN YOUR FUR.

I switched off the TV set.

"I've seen enough!" I said. "This is a ripoff. What a dirty trick!"

"*Tricks,*" Pamela said. "Veronica stole the idea of an animal video. Then she stole the whole routine."

Pamela scratched her head. "But how

did she *do* it? How did she steal all those ideas? How did she know *exactly* what Duz was doing on *his* video?"

6

Pamela was looking at me for answers.

All I could say was "We had guards. We had top security."

"Maybe somebody on the set told her," Pamela said. "A cameraman...the director..."

"No," I said. "Zero trusted all the people he hired. He said they were okay. He said they would keep it secret."

"Well, then, maybe Veronica slipped in. Maybe we didn't notice her," Pamela said.

"Nah. Everybody there had a job to do. Nobody was just hanging around."

"A job to do," Pamela said. "A *job...*"

She was smiling.

"What, what?" I asked.

"Delivering dog food is a job," she said. "Remember the guy who walked in? He was wearing a CALL-A-KIBBLE jacket and cap. Ever hear of CALL-A-KIBBLE?"

I shrugged. "I've heard of take-out pizza and Chinese food and stuff like that. I didn't know there was fast food for dogs."

"Let's look in the phone books," Pamela said. "Look under anything doggy."

Pamela and I got a bunch of phone books. We looked through all of them.

There was no CALL-A-KIBBLE.

Pamela made a face. "I bet that our doggy delivery guy was *Veronica.* Her hair must have been tucked under that cap.

She was dressed in a guy's outfit. She looked like a guy."

"But she left," I said.

"Wanna bet? Maybe she pretended to leave. She probably hid out and watched Duz do everything. She saw, she listened, she *copied!*"

"But somebody would have seen her."

"If anybody saw her, well, she was just the delivery guy, maybe waiting to deliver his food later."

"What about that CALL-A-KIBBLE outfit?"

"Easy enough to make. She just sewed some letters on a jacket."

"Hey, maybe you're onto something," I said. "But I don't know. We can't be sure."

"No, we can't," Pamela said. "If only we could *prove* it."

Pamela gritted her teeth.

"There must be a way," I said. "Everybody saw her."

"*Her?* They saw a delivery guy. And just because there was a fake name, well, how do we connect that to Veronica?"

"So this is a dead end?" I said. "We think we know how Veronica stole the video idea. But we can't prove it."

"That's right," Pamela said. "I'm so *mad!* I'm so mad I could eat a cat!"

"You don't mean that, right?"

Pamela licked her lips.

We told my parents and Ms. Muddlewolf about Veronica and CALL-A-KIBBLE. We tried to tell Zero. But we couldn't find him.

His secretary said he was on a "quest." That's all she would say.

"I bet he's still trying to come up with something to promote Duz's video," I said.

"You mean that immortal Hollywood legend stuff?" Pamela said. "Sounds good. But didn't Zero try everything when Duz was running for an Oscar? He got Duz loads of interviews. I mean, what could

Zero do now that he didn't do before?"

"Well, he couldn't get Duz on the *Babs Whoppers* show. She turned him down. She said she was all booked up with presidents and kings."

"Yeah, she gets the most famous people on earth on her show. And there's really quite a few kings around, so don't feel bad about your dog," Pamela said.

Another week went by. Then one night at midnight, the phone rang.

It was Zero. No surprise. He loves midnight.

"Great, great news!" he said. "Have you ever heard of Queen Drabia of Flabia?"

"Well, there are so many new countries lately..."

"Listen, Queen Drabia has the flu! Fabulous, fabulous flu. And—"

"And?" I asked.

"And just call her Queen No-Show. She was supposed to go on the *Babs Whoppers* show on Friday. Babs was going to interview her at the royal castle."

"Castle?"

"Yes. But the queen's too sick. So guess who's taking her place."

"You mean…"

"I do. Fred, this is the show of Hollywood legends. The show of presidents and kings. And now the show of Duz Shedd. On Friday, Babs Whoppers is coming to *your* house."

"I'm scared," I said. "Will she expect a moat and a drawbridge?"

8

We had an emergency meeting—right then and there—in the middle of the night. Zero, me, Pamela, my parents. And, of course, Duz.

First I told Zero about Veronica and CALL-A-KIBBLE.

"That lady outfoxed us. Outcatted us. Whatever!" he said. "But we can't worry about that now. We must go forward. The *Babs Whoppers* show is more important than ever. Duz's appearance on it must be perfect. Now, does everybody understand the word 'perfect'?"

We all nodded. Duz barked.

"So, tell me, what could go wrong?" Zero said. "Now is the time to tell me."

Pamela raised her hand. "What if Babs asks Duz for his famous look of longing?"

Zero beckoned to Duz. "Duz, your look of longing, please."

A big, dreamy smile spread across Duz's face.

"There you go," Zero said. "He can do it."

"But sometimes he needs to see or smell baloney to do it," I said. "And that's a secret."

"Well, figure something out. Next problem?"

Everyone was quiet. "Nothing else?" Zero asked. "Good. This dog is a star. He will wow Babs Whoppers. He will wow

America. He will sell videos."

Zero yawned. "Now it's time for me to get some sleep."

"You sleep?" Pamela said. "I wasn't sure about that."

"Tonight we will all sleep well," Zero said. "And look forward to a perfect show."

9

Some perfect. The very next day we got bad news. I mean, really bad news.

Zero called us. "A glitch," he said.

"You mean a titch of a glitch? A tiny one?" I asked.

"Well, perhaps 'glitch' isn't the right word," Zero said. "Try *disaster.*"

"Disaster?"

"Babs Whoppers wants to put Veronica and her cat on the show, too."

"What? It's supposed to be Duz's show."

"Well, it will be. But Babs thought she

should give a few minutes to the rival video. Just have Veronica and her cat sort of drop in and drop out."

"I will not let Veronica and her cat into my house," I said. "No way! Forget the show. Forget Babs Whoppers."

Zero groaned. "Without this show, Duz's video will go down the drain. Do you want that? Your dog worked his tail off for this video."

"This is awful," I said. "I lose either way."

"Call me back. Let me know what you want to do. But first repeat over and over...*down the drain, down the drain.*" Zero hung up.

I called Pamela. She rushed right over. I told her what Zero had said.

Pamela walked around and around the room. Back and forth, back and forth.

"What are you doing?" I asked.

"Thinking," she said.

"Nothing to think about," I said. "This is a no-win."

"Maybe not," she said. "Maybe not."

Pamela sat down.

"Listen to this," she said. "It's kind of weird. It could backfire. *But...*"

10

I told Zero yes.

I didn't tell him why.

I didn't tell him that Pamela had a plan.

Would the plan work?

It was a real gamble.

I was scared.

And it blew my mind just knowing that Babs Whoppers was coming to my house.

It must have blown everybody's mind. There were constant TV spots announcing it. There were headlines. A blimp with a DUZ-BABS banner flew over California.

We had to get ready.

Duz's butler and maid, Charles and Diana, dashed around our house, making it shiny and clean.

At eleven o'clock on Friday, a bunch of TV people arrived to set things up.

One of them kept staring at Duz. "Babs has never interviewed a dog. Does he talk?"

Another scratched his head. "I don't get this," he said. "I mean, what can this dog *do* for twenty minutes?"

"Duz has a lot of talent," I said. "And he's nice."

Duz wagged his tail.

My parents looked worried.

A woman walked up to them. "Just relax. Babs wants to show the world the real Duz. You've seen her interviews. The movie stars sit around in jeans and old shirts."

"Duz doesn't have any of those," I said. "But he has his Genghis Khan costume."

"Or he could wear his very lovely diamond collar," my mother said.

"No, no, NO!" the woman said. "We'll have none of that."

She motioned to one of the men. "Vases of flowers. We need them here and here and here."

She pointed and pointed and pointed. Flowers appeared from nowhere.

Suddenly the woman was gone. So were the men.

My mother looked around. "Where's Pamela? Why isn't she here? She's *always* here."

"Pamela is going to sneak in through the back door later," I explained. "We don't want the cameras to see her now."

"Why not?" my father asked.

"Never mind," my mother said. "If you told me, it might make me even more nervous. Although I don't know how I could be. I've got Babs Whoppers coming to my house. And then that horrible cat lady is coming. I'd love to slam the door in that cat lady's face!"

I smiled.

At a quarter to two, Babs Whoppers arrived. She was wearing a suit and a lot of jewelry.

Duz sniffed her.

My mother whispered to my father, "That's a diamond collar she's wearing. So why couldn't Duz wear his?"

"Shh," my father said.

Babs shook hands with my parents and me. Then she swooped down on Duz.

"Ah, the star," she said.

Duz kept sniffing.

More people arrived. With cameras and lights and stuff. They wandered in and out of rooms. So did Babs.

Suddenly the buzzing and moving around stopped. We were ready. This was live television. We were now open to the eyes and ears of the world!

The interview began.

"I am in the Hollywood residence of America's newest—and bushiest—star," Babs said. "Duz Shedd, known to his legions of fans as Genghis Khan."

Duz raised an ear.

"When Duz takes off his Genghis costume—his goggles, his motorcycle jacket, his boots—what is he *really* like?

Relaxing at home. Enjoying his hobbies."

Duz was lying on the floor, doing nothing.

"Duz lives here with his family, Mr. and Mrs. Shedd and their son, Fred."

Suddenly Babs was on the floor, staring at Duz.

"My, you really *are* ugly-looking, aren't you," she said.

"Extremely," my father said proudly.

Babs was still eyeballing Duz.

"Duz, could you show us how you live? Could you give us a tour of your dog house?"

Duz wagged his tail. He ran to his bedroom. He leaped onto his bed.

Everybody followed.

"A bone-shaped bed!" Babs said. "I should have known."

Duz leaped off the bed. Then he led the way around the rest of the house.

He stopped at his dog bowls.

The cameras zoomed in on them.

"Charming house," Babs said. "But where do you keep your Oscar?"

Duz led the way back to his bedroom.

He sniffed under the bed.

I spoke up. "Duz likes to sleep with his Oscar close by. So he keeps it under his bed."

"Logical," Babs murmured.

Duz led the way back to the living room. Then he jumped up on a chair. Babs sat down in a chair across from him.

She looked him straight in the eye.

"Well, now I have some really tough questions for you, Duz. You had humble beginnings. And now you're rich. How does that *feel?*"

I spoke up. "What are humble beginnings?"

Babs looked annoyed.

"It means Duz was a stray," my father whispered.

"Duz was great right from the start," I said.

"Of course," Babs said. "We'll go on to another question. Duz, how did it feel to be kidnapped?"

I butted in. "Duz can't answer that," I said. "He has a book contract. He'll tell all about the kidnapping in his book. You'll have to read about it there."

"But it could not have been pleasant

being kidnapped by the cat lady," Babs said. "Duz, at least give us one teensy quote about that."

Babs went nose to nose with Duz.

She waited.

Duz growled.

"Ah, the quote I wanted," she said. "An exclusive."

Babs seemed happy.

But then her voice got serious. It scared me.

"Now let's talk career. Duz, you are a very special actor."

Duz looked right at Babs, as if he were under her spell.

"It's time, Duz," she said.

"Time for what?" I asked.

"For Duz to show the world that famous Duz look of longing. The look that says more than words can ever say."

Oh, no! What if Duz couldn't do it without baloney!

Babs kept staring at him. "Duz, I'm waiting. The whole world is waiting…"

Duz seemed to be in a trance. Maybe Babs had an evil eye. I had to do something fast.

I walked up to Babs. I tapped her on the shoulder. "Um…I bet you're hungry."

I rushed into the kitchen before Babs could answer. I was back in a few seconds with food.

"Have a baloney sandwich, Babs."

"Our baloney is the best," my mother said.

"I'm sure it is," Babs said. "But I asked Duz…"

"For the look of longing," I said. "And

there it is."

Duz had his famous look! His eyes, his nose, his mouth—his entire face had changed. He was practically drooling for the baloney I was holding beside Babs.

"I'm impressed," Babs said. "This dog's timing is perfect. He waited for the suspense to build up before he gave me the look. What a clever dog. What an actor!"

What a baloney lover, I thought.

And now Duz was waiting for his reward. To eat the baloney.

Babs wasn't eating.

"You hate baloney," I said to Babs. "I can tell."

"Well…"

"We never waste food around here," I said. I gave Babs's sandwich to Duz. He chomped it down.

"I love a family that recycles," Babs said.

My parents were beaming. Everything was going great.

Suddenly the doorbell rang.

Good-bye, great.

I knew who was out there.

It was time for Veronica Slye.

11

The cameras were focused on the door.

For Veronica Slye's entrance with Geca.

Babs announced, "We have visitors. Fred, would you and Duz like to answer the door?"

"I'll get the door," a voice called.

Pamela ran into the room.

Everyone gasped when they saw her. Except me. I knew just what she would look like.

She was wearing a cap that had CALL-A-KIBBLE printed on it.

She winked at me and rushed to the door. She flung it open.

Veronica Slye was standing there.

Her cat was sitting on her shoulder.

The cameras moved in for a closeup of Veronica and Geca.

Veronica was smiling. She was thrilled to be on Babs Whoppers' program. She was thrilled to worm her way onto Duz's show. She was prepared to wreck it.

It was a short thrill.

Veronica looked at Pamela.

Pamela cheerfully tipped her cap.

"Hi, there!" Pamela said. "Did you call for dog food?"

"How did you...?" began Veronica.

"We know everything," Pamela said. "And now the whole world does."

Pamela turned to the cameramen. "You

got all of this, right?"

The cameramen nodded.

Pamela said, "Babs?"

Babs nodded, too.

They had no idea what they were getting. They had no idea what was going on.

But Veronica didn't know that.

Her face turned red.

She looked at Babs. "You set this up. A trap! So what if I hid out and stole the idea for Duz's video? So what if I copied it for my cat? Do you have a cat?"

"I have a rabbit," Babs said.

"No talent there," Veronica huffed. "My Geca here is a big talent. She should have been a movie star. Instead, this...this... mutt got an Oscar."

Veronica's face got redder.

Duz went to the door. He started to growl.

Veronica went on, "Was movie stardom enough for this dog? No. He had to become a *video* star."

Pamela tipped her cap again.

"Thank you for that worldwide confession," she said.

Then she slammed the door in Veronica's face.

Babs went up to Pamela. "Could you fill the viewers in on what just happened?"

"Gladly," Pamela said.

She cleared her throat.

"Veronica pretended to be a dog-food delivery person. She got in to the taping of Duz's video. She saw it all. Then she copied all the ideas to make a video for her cat. That's it. And now I bet everyone is anxious to see a sample of *Duz's* video."

I held my breath. Pamela was telling Babs how to run her show.

But we had to advertise the video.

"Of course," Babs said.

My father turned on the music. "Do the Duzzy."

Duz began to thump, bump, wiggle, and jiggle.

Pamela hugged me.

"What a happy ending!" my mother whispered to my father.

The song kept going. *"Wag that tail! Fetch that mail!"*

Duz wagged his tail.

Then he looked at Babs's shoes.

So did I. But it was too late.

Babs's shoes were beautiful. All shiny and new and tasseled.

Duz lunged for them.

He grabbed one in his teeth.

He pulled. So did Babs. The shoe split in two.

Duz proudly brought half a shoe to me.

Babs stood there. One shoe on, one

shoe off. "I bought these shoes in Italy. For a thousand dollars!" she said.

"We're dead," Pamela whispered to me.

My father said, "No more fetch. Duz will stretch."

Duz started to bend and stretch.

"Never mind," Babs said. "I'll just buy the video. After I buy a new pair of shoes."

Babs sat down. She tucked her shoeless foot under her.

Duz jumped up on the chair across from her. And then, out of the blue, he gave her the look of longing.

Babs smiled.

They looked nice together. Shoe or no shoe, they were friends.

"Duz," Babs said, "I know your video

is charming. It's a shoo-in for success. Just a little pun there. The public will be lining up to buy it."

"Yay!" Pamela said under her breath.

Babs stared at Duz. "Now I have one last question for you. Superstar. Oscar winner. And just plain nice dog."

Duz wagged his tail.

"Duz," Babs said softly. "How do you want to be remembered?"

Babs always asked that question.

Duz twitched his nose. He knew there was more baloney around.

"Ah, as a nose-twitcher!" Babs said. "No one has ever given me that answer. Very original."

The show was over.

"Your dog is a wonder. A legend," Babs said as she limped out.

The next day it was in all the news-papers:

BABS MEETS GENGHIS!

The interview got the highest ratings of all of Babs's shows.

Sales of *Shape Up with Duz* went-through the roof. *Shape Up with Geca,* now known as the copycat video, was taken off the market.

It's rumored that Babs Whoppers has received 4,397 pairs of new shoes from fans.

So far.

Don't miss the first three books in the Duz Shedd series!